Five reasons why you'll love Isadora Moon...

Meet the magical,
fang-tastic Isadora Moon!

Isadora's cuddly toy, Pink Rabbit,
has been magicked to life!

Get ready for some
magical mischief!

Isadora's family is crazy!

Enchanting
pink and black
pictures

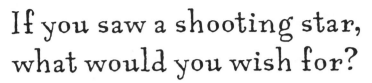

If you saw a shooting star, what would you wish for?

I wish I could ride on a dragon.
- Primrose, aged 5

I wish I could have a caticorn.
- Daniela, aged 9

I would wish to become a famous pop star!
- Lydia, aged 5

I would wish for a magical pet dinosaur who is pink.
- Harriette, aged 6

I would wish for a necklace that could turn a person into a fairy and a mermaid.
- Phoebe, aged 8

I would wish that my house was made out of sweets.
- Blaire, aged 6

I wish I could fly and go round the moon.
- Eleanor, aged 6

I would wish for pigeons with unicorn horns to ride to school on!
- Freya, aged 5

I would wish for a paddling pool with a slide from my bedroom window!
- Alice, aged 5

I wish that I could jump into an Isadora book and be Isadora's best friend for a day.
- Penelope, aged 7

I would wish it was Christmas and I could get presents every day.
- Zac, aged 5

Family Tree

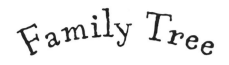

My Mum
Countess Cordelia
Moon

Baby Honeyblossom

My Dad
Count Bartholomew
Moon

Me!
Isadora Moon

Pink Rabbit

For vampires, fairies and humans everywhere!
And for my ever-stylish agent Jodie Hodges and
the team at United Agents.

OXFORD
UNIVERSITY PRESS

Great Clarendon Street, Oxford OX2 6DP
Oxford University Press is a department of the University of Oxford.
It furthers the University's objective of excellence in research, scholarship,
and education by publishing worldwide. Oxford is a registered trade mark
of Oxford University Press in the UK and in certain other countries

Text copyright © Harriet Muncaster 2021
Illustrated by Harriet Muncaster and Rob Parkinson 2021

The moral rights of the author have been asserted

Database right Oxford University Press (maker)

First published in 2021
First published in paperback 2022

British Library Cataloguing in Publication Data

Data available

ISBN:978-0-19-278345-5

3 5 7 9 10 8 6 4 2

Printed in Great Britain by Bell and Bain Ltd, Glasgow

Paper used in the production of this book is a natural,
recyclable product made from wood grown in sustainable forests.
The manufacturing process conforms to the environmental
regulations of the country of origin.

MIX
Paper from
responsible sources
FSC
www.fsc.org
FSC® C007785

ISADORA · MOON

and the Shooting Star

Harriet Muncaster

OXFORD
UNIVERSITY PRESS

Chapter ONE

It was almost home time on Monday afternoon and Miss Cherry had an announcement.

'Tomorrow, we are going to start a project on space!' she said. 'We are going to learn all about the night sky.'

'Ooh!' said the class and I saw my friend Bruno punch the air. He loves

anything to do with space. Even his
lunchbox has pictures of aliens on it.

'Most excitingly,' Miss Cherry continued, 'we are going to have a visit from the famous astronomer, Astrid Luna. She is going to come and talk to us all about the stars and planets!'

'Oh, wow!' yelled Bruno, jumping up from his chair.

'Sit down please Bruno,' said Miss Cherry.

'To go alongside our project,' she continued, 'I am going to set you some homework which you can start thinking about tonight. I want each one of you to make something to do with space. It can be anything you like. Be creative! You can have the rest of the week to work on it.'

'Oh, yay!' said my best friend Zoe who was sitting next to me. 'I know what I'm going to do already. I'm going to paint a huge starry picture of the Milky Way with lots of glitter on it! What are you going to do Isadora?'

'I'm not sure,' I said as I packed up my pencil case. 'I'm going to think about it tonight. We don't have to start it yet.'

'*I'm* going to start mine tonight,' said Bruno. 'It's going to take me ages. I want to make a whole solar system from papier mâché with aliens and everything!'

'I'm going to start mine tonight too,' said Sashi. 'I want to make a rocket out of cardboard and silver foil!'

I stared round at my friends as we all packed up our bags to go home and felt just the tiniest bit panicked. I didn't have any idea of what to make for the special project and now I couldn't make a cardboard rocket or a papier mâché solar system or paint a starry picture because it would look like I was copying my friends. I needed to think of something else.

I'll ask Dad to help, I thought as I walked out into the playground. He loves astronomy.

Dad was VERY excited to hear about my school project. His favourite hobby is stargazing and he has a special telescope set up in the window of the second tallest turret in our house. He can spend all night stargazing! Luckily, he's a vampire so he has no trouble staying awake all night while me, Mum, and my baby sister Honeyblossom are asleep.

'I can help you with the project Isadora,' he said. 'You should stay up and stargaze with me this evening. It's going to be a clear night!'

'I suppose you could stay up late,' said Mum. 'As it's for a school project.'

Pink Rabbit bounced up and down beside me with excitement. He used to

be my favourite stuffed toy but my mum magicked him alive with her wand. She can do things like that because she's a fairy.

'I also have to make something to do with space,' I said. 'But I can't think of anything. All my friends have already decided what they're doing.'

'How about making a rocket out of cardboard and tin foil?' suggested Dad.

'Sashi's making that,' I said. 'I don't want to copy.'

'How about one of those solar system mobiles with all the planets hanging down on strings?' suggested Mum.

'Bruno's doing a solar system,' I said. 'I want to do something different.'

'Hmm,' said Mum.

'You'll think of something,' said Dad.

That evening, Dad and I wrapped ourselves in a blanket and sat in front of the telescope in the astronomy tower. The sky outside was dark and glittering all over with stars.

'Aren't they beautiful!' said Dad. 'That big bright one over there is Venus. And look! There's a shooting star!'

I only had time to look at it for a second before Dad said 'Look! There's another! It's even brighter than the last one.'

I turned my head to look and both
Dad and I stared in wonder as a bright
spot of light whizzed across the sky,
getting lower and lower all the time.

'That's funny,' said Dad, 'It looks like

it's falling to Earth!' He quickly put his eye to the telescope.

'It IS falling to Earth!' he exclaimed. 'I've never seen that happen before. Isadora, have a look!'

I peered into the telescope and watched as the bright star fell down, down, down. It was falling right OUT of the night sky!

'It looks like it's going to land on the other side of town!' said Dad jumping up. 'Astonishing! Come on Isadora, let's go and find it!'

Chapter TWO

I felt an excited fizzing in my chest as I raced down the stairs after Dad and grabbed my coat from the peg in the hallway. Dad wrenched open the front door and we stepped out into the milky moonlight. It was a chilly night and I shivered.

'I hope no one else finds it before we

do,' said Dad as he took my hand.

'I'm sure they won't,' I reassured him. 'Humans will all be asleep at this time.'

Together, we rose up into the air. Dad's black cape swirled out behind him and I flapped my little bat wings. We soared up, up until we were high above the town. The houses looked like tiny black squares and the rows of lamp posts along the roads became strings of glowing pearls in the darkness.

'Keep a lookout Isadora,' said Dad.
'The star landed somewhere to the north!'
We flew over the town square, the
high street, and the shops. I recognized
the duck pond glinting like a silver penny
in the moonlight.

Soon we reached the edge of town where there were just a few houses and then fields and a forest beyond. I squinted my eyes hard. Where could the fallen star be?

'I can't see it Dad,' I said after a few minutes.

'Nor can I,' said Dad, sounding disappointed. 'Maybe it's further north.'

We continued to fly over the forest, the fields, and dark country lanes, but there was no sign of the star. What if it wasn't a star we saw at all? Visions of strange and frightening looking aliens started to dance though my mind and suddenly I wasn't sure I wanted to go

looking for the 'star' after all.

'Dad,' I said, pulling at his hand. 'I want to go home!'

'Home?' said Dad, sounding surprised. 'Why?'

'I . . .' I began, and then I stopped.

What was that?

Down below us, emerging from a bush at the side of a dark country lane was a small glowy thing. I stared at it in horror and then in wonder. Was this what we had seen falling from the sky? It didn't look like a star exactly, or a scary alien! It looked soft and magical and twinkly.

'Dad!' I whispered. 'Look!'

'Ooh!' said Dad.

We both gazed downwards as
the 'star' moved slowly down the lane,
stopping every now and then when it
came to a bush. It seemed to be looking for
something. Suddenly, it turned around and
started walking back the other way.

'I think it might be lost,' I said to
Dad. 'Maybe we should see if we can
help?'

'I think that's a good idea,' said Dad.

'But let's be quiet and gentle. We don't want to startle it.'

We flew a little way up the country lane and landed round a corner from where the 'star' was.

Together we started to walk, our footsteps crunching on the path.

'It's a jolly nice night for a walk!' said Dad in a very friendly sort of voice.

'Yes!' I agreed loudly. 'It is!'

'We're just two extremely nice people out for a midnight ramble,' continued Dad, as we rounded the corner, just in time to see the 'star' scurrying into a bush at the side of the lane. It was hard for the 'star' to hide though. We could still see its light, shining out from among the branches.

'Don't be frightened,' called out Dad. 'We won't hurt you! We just wanted to check you were all right.'

'Yes,' I agreed. 'We saw you falling from the sky!'

'You did?' came a voice from inside the bush, and then a glowy hand appeared through the branches.

'Nice to meet you,' I said, taking the hand and shaking it. 'I'm Isadora Moon and this is my dad!'

'My name's Nova,' came the voice

again and suddenly there was a cracking
of twigs and a rustling of leaves as Nova
stuck her head out of the bush and stepped
cautiously out. She had two antennae
sticking out from the top of her head with
little twinkly stars on the top and skin
that glowed and shimmered all over. She

was so bright that I had to squint a bit to look at her.

'Wow!' I said. 'We thought you were a shooting star.'

'A star?' giggled Nova. 'I'm not a star, I'm a Glow Sprite!'

'A Glow Sprite?' I said. 'Well, I've never seen a Glow Sprite either!'

'We often get mistaken for shooting stars,' said Nova. 'We play among the planets in the night sky!'

'Really?' said Dad. 'That's VERY interesting! I've never read about Glow Sprites in any of my astronomy books. Which planet do you live on?'

'It's called Glistopia,' said Nova. 'It

looks just like a normal star when you're looking at it from Earth. The night sky is our playground but we hardly ever come close to Earth . . . well, we're not supposed to anyway in case humans see us.' Nova started to wring her hands, worriedly. 'Oh, I'm going to be in so much trouble if he's lost on Earth!'

'Who?' I asked.

'My moon kitten, Pluto,' said Nova. 'We were playing chase together, whizzing across the night sky, but he came a little too close to Earth and disappeared. I saw him fall out of the sky and land somewhere around here. But I can't find him anywhere!'

'Oh!' said Dad. 'We did see another shooting star just before we spotted you but we didn't notice where it landed. We were so busy looking at *you* through the telescope!'

'Oh no!' wailed Nova, and suddenly she burst into loud noisy sobs. Sparkling tears of stardust ran down her cheeks and splashed glitteringly onto the ground.

'Don't be upset Nova!' I said, putting my arm around her. 'We'll help you find your moon kitten. He can't be far away if you said he fell somewhere near to here.'

'Yes,' agreed Dad, 'and if he's as glowy as you then we'll be sure to find him in no time.' He reached into his cape

and pulled out a large bat patterned
handkerchief which he held out to Nova.
She took it and blew her nose.

'I hope Pluto is OK,' she sniffed.

'I'm sure he's fine,' said Dad
reassuringly. 'Let's start looking right
away. Come on!'

Chapter
THREE

Dad shot into the air with his black cape flying out behind him and I held my hand out to Nova. She took it and we flew up into the air too, following Dad who looked like a giant bat flapping in the darkness.

'Pluto definitely fell somewhere near this town!' said Nova. 'I just didn't see exactly where!'

'Look for anything glowy!' shouted Dad. 'Keep your eyes peeled!'

I stared down at the dark fields and the forest below, straining to try and spot anything that might look like a moon kitten. But all I could see was darkness and the occasional headlight from a car winding along the country lane.

'It's useless,' said Nova after a while. 'We're never going to find Pluto!' and she

started to cry again.

'It IS more difficult than I thought,' said Dad, as we hovered in the air above a clump of trees. 'But he will be somewhere. We're just not looking in the right place.'

'What if we NEVER look in the right place!' said Nova. 'I can't go back home without him! Mum will be so cross!'

'She must be worried!' I said thinking about how I would feel if Pink Rabbit had gone missing.

'She will be if we're not home by tomorrow evening,' said Nova. 'Pluto and I often stay out playing with our friends all night long. Mum's used to that. The sky is perfectly safe for young Glow Sprites and their pets as long as we stay close to Glistopia. But if we're not back by the time she gets home from work at the Stardust Factory tomorrow evening then I'm going to be in big, big trouble!'

'Hmm,' said Dad.

'Why don't you come back to our house, Nova?' I suggested. 'Maybe, if we get some sleep, we can think of a better plan in the morning!' Then I had a sudden thought.

'There's a famous astronomer coming to visit our school tomorrow,' I said. 'Maybe she will be able to help! She might know something about how to find a lost moon kitten.'

Nova looked doubtful.

'I'm not sure,' she said. 'Most humans don't know anything about us.'

'Well even if she doesn't,' I said. 'She's an astronomer. She probably studies the night sky all the time! Maybe she was looking through her telescope last night and spotted where Pluto landed!'

'Maybe . . .' said Nova, starting to look a bit more hopeful. She wiped

her eyes and put the bat patterned
handkerchief into her pocket.

'I AM quite tired,' she said. 'Maybe it
would be better to begin our search again
in the morning.'

Nova, Dad and I flew home. By the time we got back to the house it was very, very late, but after all our flying and searching we were hungry.

'Cheese toasties are what you need Nova,' said Dad. 'They'll make you feel better for sure!' and he started to cut and butter some bread, which was very nice of him, as I know Dad hates touching any food that isn't red.

'Have you had cheese before Nova?' I asked.

'Oh yes,' Nova nodded. 'We have the best cheese in the universe in space! Moon cheese!'

Dad finished making our toasties

and we gobbled them down with a glass
of milk. Nova seemed a lot more cheerful
after that.

'We WILL find
Pluto,' she said, as I

led her up the stairs to my bedroom. 'I know it! He's got lost a few times before, but I always do find him in the end. He likes playing hide and seek a little too much sometimes. He's cheeky!'

'Of course we'll find him!' I said reassuringly. 'Let's get some sleep. We'll be able to think more clearly tomorrow.'

'OK,' smiled Nova, and sat down on the edge of my bed as I rummaged beneath it to find my special portable fairy mattress. It's hard to find as it's so small and

there's a lot of
mess under my
bed! Eventually
I found it
behind a dusty
box of dollshouse
furniture.

'Here's your bed Nova!'
I said, holding up a tiny pouch.

Nova looked confused so I opened
the pouch and pulled out a tiny fluffy pink
cloud. As soon as it was in the air the
cloud began to grow, puffing bigger and
bigger until it was the size of a double
mattress.

'Wow!' said Nova, leaping onto it.

'This is so soft and bouncy! It's just like the clouds in the sky!'

'I know,' I said. 'It's supposed to be for sleepovers but sometimes I sleep on it just for fun!'

Then I found Nova a spare pair

of pyjamas and we went down to the bathroom to brush our teeth.

At last we both crawled into our beds and I turned out the light.

'Goodnight Isadora,' said Nova and snuggled down into the pink cloud, closing her eyes.

'Goodnight,' I whispered. But I didn't close my eyes because something felt really different in my bedroom. I had turned out my lamp and closed the curtains, but it was still so light! It was Nova, giving off her bright glow.

'Oh dear,' I whispered to Pink Rabbit.

'I can't sleep in such a bright room!' I pulled the duvet up over my head but it got too stuffy so in the end I snuck downstairs and asked Dad for one of his special lightproof vampire eye masks.

'That's better,' I whispered as I pulled it down over my eyes. 'Goodnight Pink Rabbit.'

Chapter FOUR

Mum was surprised to see Nova at breakfast the next morning.

'A Glow Sprite?' she said. 'How interesting! And what do Glow Sprites eat for breakfast?'

'Oh, just anything really,' said Nova politely. 'Astro loops or Comet Crunchies or Star Nuggets with moon milk . . .'

'Ah,' said Mum.

'How about some peanut

butter on toast like Isadora?'

'OK!' said Nova excitedly.

Over breakfast Nova told us all about

what it was like to be a Glow Sprite.

'We can whizz across the sky really

fast,' she explained. 'We're

supposed to stay near

Glistopia if Mum's not with us but Pluto is naughty sometimes and tries to go further. He's always whizzing off and hiding amongst the planets. He's never actually landed on one before though.'

'It sounds fun!' I said.

'It is,' said Nova. 'Maybe you can come and visit my house on Glistopia one day Isadora. It's quite cold though, you'll have to wrap up warm. Glow Sprites don't really get affected by the weather. Also, there's not much gravity there. You'll float!'

'I'm not sure about that,' said Mum quickly.

'Is there oxygen?' asked Dad.

'Oh no,' said Nova cheerfully. 'Glow Sprites don't need oxygen!'

'*Mmm*,' I said, not wanting to hurt Nova's feelings. I was absolutely sure I never wanted to visit Glistopia. Space sounded so . . . BIG! I liked my cosy house with Mum and Dad on planet Earth.

After breakfast, Nova and I went back upstairs to get ready for school. I couldn't wait to get there so we could ask Astrid Luna if she had spotted a star falling from the sky last night. Now that it was daylight, Nova wasn't glowing so much.

'Hopefully no one will notice that I'm

different,' said Nova as she pulled one of my hats down over her head to hide her starry antennae.

'Why?' I asked. 'It's OK to be different you know. I'm a vampire fairy, which is very different from all my human friends. You should be proud to be a Glow Sprite!'

'Oh, I am!' said Nova. 'But humans aren't really supposed to know much about us. We don't want them sending out spaceships to investigate Glistopia! I need to stay in disguise. Humans are bad and dangerous.'

'Are they?' I asked. I had always found humans to be quite friendly.

'Yes,' said Nova. 'All Glow Sprites are taught that from an early age! I'd be far too frightened to let them see me without my disguise.'

When we arrived at school there was much excitement and chattering going on in the classroom.

'Astrid Luna will be here this afternoon,' said Miss Cherry. 'Sit down everyone please! Ah, this must be Nova. Isadora, your mum did inform me she'd be joining our class just for today.'

As I walked towards my desk I could see that lots of my friends had already started their space project. Zoe had a half-finished painting sitting in front of her and Sashi had brought in a cardboard rocket, painted silver. Bruno had lots of big round balls of different sizes sitting on his desk. I guessed they were going to be

planets in his solar system. Once again, I felt a little zing of panic in my tummy. I still hadn't thought of anything to make for the project!

I sat down at my desk with Nova next to me and tried to concentrate on the first lesson, but it was hard. My mind kept wandering to whether Mum and Dad had found Pluto yet. They had promised they would go and search for him straight after breakfast, while Nova and I were at school. I think Nova was wondering the same thing, as she wouldn't stop fidgeting next to me.

At break time all my friends swarmed over to us in the playground. They were all very interested in Nova.

'Where are you from?' asked Zoe.

'Why are you wearing your hat inside?' asked Oliver.

'Is your skin GLOWING?' asked Samantha. 'I love it! It's so sparkly!'

At first Nova looked frightened. She tried to answer the questions as best as she could without revealing that she was a Glow Sprite. But by the end of break time she was smiling.

'See! Not all humans are bad and dangerous,' I whispered.

'No,' agreed Nova. 'They're just like you and me!'

Even so, Nova refused to take off her disguise.

'I'll be in big trouble back on Glistopia if I reveal myself to humans,' she said.

After lunch, once we were all sitting back at our desks, the classroom door opened, and the head teacher poked her head around it.

'Astrid Luna is here!' she said.

Immediately, excited chattering started up in the classroom again and this time Miss Cherry didn't even try to stop it. I could tell she was excited too because her cheeks had gone all pink.

'Welcome Astrid Luna!' she said as a tall lady came into the classroom. She was wearing lots of starry jewellery and had two big moon shaped earrings swinging

from her ears. She perched herself on the edge of Miss Cherry's desk and beamed round at us all.

'Good morning!' she said.

'Good morning Astrid Luna,' we chanted, and then there was silence. We all wanted to hear what Astrid Luna had to say. She was mesmerizing.

Astrid Luna began to talk. She told us all about the planets and the Milky Way and star constellations. She opened up her suitcase and got out a big telescope and let us have a look through it. She showed us photographs of strange and wonderful things and models of spaceships.

'Space really is beautiful,' she said. 'And vast! We've probably only discovered a teeny tiny amount of what is actually out there! Did you know for example that somewhere in the Universe, there may be a planet made of diamonds?'

'There is!' whispered Nova into my ear. 'I've seen it!'

'There are many, many things we still don't know about space,' continued Astrid Luna. 'And that's what's so exciting about it! Now does anyone have any questions?'

Bruno's hand immediately shot up into the air.

'Astrid Luna,' he said. 'Are there aliens in space?'

The class laughed but Astrid Luna looked serious.

'There could well be!' she said. 'In fact, I believe there must surely be life on a planet somewhere, maybe in a different solar system, or maybe even in our solar system!'

'Wow!' said Bruno, and he looked

really happy.

Some of my other classmates put
up their hands and asked questions too.
I knew this was my moment, but I felt
nervous. Tentatively I put up my hand.

'Yes?' smiled Astrid Luna.

'Erm . . .' I began. 'I was just
WONDERING if you saw a shooting star
fall to Earth last night?'

'Not last night,'
laughed Astrid
Luna. 'I didn't
stargaze. I was
busy preparing
this presentation!
Why do you ask?

Shooting stars don't usually fall to Earth.'

'Don't they?' I said.

Astrid Luna frowned, and I could see the rest of the class looking round at me confused. I felt my face go red.

'There is ONE legend,' said Astrid Luna. 'But I'm surprised you know about it. Not many people have heard of the Glow Sprites.'

'Oh,' I said. 'Is THAT what they're called?'

'Yes,' said Astrid Luna. 'They look like shooting stars! The story goes that once, a long, long time ago, a Glow Sprite fell to Earth and was seen up close by an astronomer. He claims

to have spoken to the Glow Sprite and that's how we know a little bit about them. But there is no evidence that they exist and so no one knows for sure whether the legend is true. Stars do sometimes look as though they're falling to Earth though, so it is a lovely story.'

'Ooh!' said the class.

A wistful look came over Astrid Luna's face.

'If the legend IS true,' she said. 'Then I would SO love to see one!'

Before I could ask any more questions about Glow Sprites, Oliver jumped up from his seat without putting up his hand.

'I'VE seen a Glow Sprite!' he

announced.

'HAVE you?' asked Astrid Luna, sounding interested.

'Sit down please Oliver,' said Miss Cherry.

Oliver sat back down but shuffled excitedly in his chair.

'Last night!' he said. 'I was looking through a telescope at the sky—for our space project. I saw TWO shooting stars fall to Earth! I DID think it was quite strange. One fell near some fields and the other one looked as though it fell right in the middle of the forest, on the edge of town!'

'How fascinating!' said Astrid Luna. 'I wish I'd seen that! Maybe you really did see a Glow Sprite! I'm very jealous! I'll have to study the sky closely tonight!'

I stared at Nova and she stared back at me.

'The forest!' we whispered together.

Chapter FIVE

As soon as the bell rang for the end of the day, Nova and I ran out of school to find both Mum and Dad waiting for us in the playground, which was unusual. They both looked worried.

'I'm afraid we haven't found Pluto yet . . .' began Mum.

'We know where he is!' I cried,

interrupting. 'He's in the forest!'

'The forest?' said Mum. 'Well then, we must go there right now! We'll drop by the house and pack some things on the way!'

'Pack some things?' asked Dad as he hurried us all into the car. 'Why?'

'We might need camping gear,' said

Mum. 'We don't know how long we'll be in the forest for, do we? It might take a while to find Pluto and it will get dark early. I'll pack the tent just in case.'

'*The tent?!*' said Dad, horrified. 'But we can just drive back home to bed. It's not THAT far to the forest. You know I hate camping!'

'Well this is an emergency and I think we should pack the tent,' said Mum.

An hour later we arrived at the edge of the forest. Mum parked the car in a layby.

'Everyone must wear a rucksack!' she said, opening the boot and handing them

out. 'There's a survival kit inside each one
and a whistle in case you get lost. There
are snacks in there too!'

We all walked towards an opening
in the trees. The path looked thin and
winding.

'It's quite dark in there,' remarked
Mum, peering in.

'Good!' said Dad who was wearing

his daytime sunglasses. 'I like the gloom!
Better for my sensitive vampire eyes.'

Nova and I held hands as we stepped
onto the path.

'It's an awfully big forest,' said Nova
in a small voice.

I squeezed her hand.

'We'll find Pluto!' I said. 'We have to!'

We started to search, walking in and out
of the trees and looking in every nook,
cranny and bush that we could find but
there was so sign of a little moon kitten
anywhere.

'I can't remember if I've looked here

yet or not,' said Dad peering into a hollow log. 'Everything looks the same. There are so many trees!'

'We're never going to find Pluto!' wailed Nova.

'Do you think he might have gone home already?' I asked.

'No,' said Nova. 'He wouldn't know the way.'

'We mustn't give up!' said Mum.

By now the sky was beginning to darken and Nova was lighting the way with her glowing skin.

'I don't think we've been down this path yet,' said Mum, pointing to a winding route that led through some brambles. She began to pick her way through it and I followed with Nova and Dad, shivering as I looked around. Suddenly, everything felt very creepy now that it was dark. I don't usually mind the dark—I am half vampire after all, but the rustling of the leaves all around felt a bit too spooky. I shivered and held on tightly to Pink Rabbit as I watched my family and Nova peer into trees and under bushes. At least I could see Nova. She was so bright. Pluto must be almost as bright too! But it was going to take a long time to find him searching on the ground. The forest was so big. I flapped my wings and rose up into the air, breaking out through the branches.

From up in the
starry sky I
could see the
whole forest.
There was one
bright spot of
light down below
where Nova was glowing
and . . . was that another, fainter one a

little way away? Could it be . . .?

My heart started to race as I peered down into the trees below.

'Mum! Dad! Nova!' I yelled. 'I think I can see Pluto!'

They all shot up into the sky to join me and I pointed to a patch of faint light glowing through the branches.

'PLUTO!' gasped Nova, and whizzed towards the glow faster than I could even blink. Mum, Dad, and I followed, landing back down in the forest by a large hollow tree.

'Oh Pluto!' cried Nova. 'It *is* him!'

I peered into the little hollow of the tree and saw a cheeky, furry, glowing face peeping out. He didn't look frightened at all! He had made himself a nice little bed from leaves and he had blackberry stains all round his mouth.

'Oh Pluto, you're so naughty!' said Nova reaching up and lifting him out of the hollow of the tree. 'I'm never letting you out of my sight again!'

'Thank goodness he's safe!' said Dad.

'And not a scratch on him! Well done for spotting his glow Isadora!'

I beamed with pride as Nova hugged Pluto tight while he squirmed in her grasp.

'Well we may as well go home now,' said Dad hopefully.

'Absolutely not!' said Mum. 'Nova, before you and Pluto head home, have you got time to have a campfire with us?'

Nova glanced up at the sky. The moon was not very high.

'We've still got a bit of time before Mum gets home from work,' she said.

Chapter
SIX

Mum led us to a clearing in the forest where
there was a fallen log long enough for us to
all sit on. Then she got the tent out of her
rucksack and waved her wand. Immediately, it
sprang up in the middle of the clearing. Then
she collected some twigs and sticks and waved
her wand over them so that pink sparks rained
down and burst into a warm flickering fire.

'Lovely!' said Mum, warming her hands over it while Dad watched on in dismay. She got some vegetarian fairy sausages, marshmallows, and chocolate biscuits out of her backpack and started to make dinner for everyone.

'Mmm!' said Nova. 'That smells delicious.'

We all sat round the campfire and ate the sausages and melted the marshmallows on the end of long forks, squishing them between chocolate biscuits. I felt so happy sitting there in front of the flickering fire with my family and with my new friend Nova. We told jokes and sang songs. I could tell that even Dad was enjoying himself, though he pretended not to! When we had finished, the moon was high in the sky and all the stars were sparkling overhead.

'Pluto and I really had better get back now,' said Nova, standing up. 'Mum will be getting home from work very soon! I don't want her to worry. Thank you very much for having me and for the delicious campfire dinner! And thank you for helping me to find my moon kitten. I don't know what I'd have done without you.'

'That's quite alright,' said Dad, wrapping his vampire cape tightly around himself. 'Have a safe journey home.'

'It's been so nice getting to know you

Nova!' I said, giving her a huge hug. 'Will you visit again?'

'I'm not really supposed to,' said Nova. 'But Earth isn't as awful as I thought it would be. Your human friends are lovely and I can't wait to tell everyone back home about my new vampire-fairy friend! I'll try and send you all some moon cheese through space post!'

'Miaow!' said Pluto.

'Pluto loves moon cheese!' laughed Nova. She held onto him tightly and then closed her eyes tight. Suddenly, sparks began to fizz out from their feet and Mum, Dad, and I stood back to watch. The sparks got brighter and brighter until

suddenly Nova and Pluto shot up into the
air with stardust trailing out behind them.
They went so fast that they looked like a
blur!

Soon they were way up high,
trailing across the midnight sky, getting
smaller and smaller until they were just a
tiny sparkling dot. And then . . . nothing.

'Wow,' said Dad, impressed. 'They
can fly even faster than vampires!'

'Amazing!' said Mum.

I just gazed upwards, staring at
the spot where Nova and Pluto had

disappeared, feeling a little bit
sad that I would probably never see
them again. But I smiled at the thought
that Astrid Luna was probably looking
through her telescope at the sky tonight.

'Come on Isadora,' said Mum putting
her arm around me. 'It's time for bed.'

We all went into the tent and I
climbed into my snuggly sleeping bag
next to Honeyblossom, hugging Pink
Rabbit tight. It felt very magical to be

sleeping in a tent for the night and I fell
asleep to the sound of leaves rustling and
owls hooting.

'I think we should sleep every night
in the tent,' said Mum happily as she
dozed off.

'Absolutely not,' said Dad. 'We are
going home straight after breakfast!'

Z Z Z Z Z !

Chapter SEVEN

The following day, I was a little late to school because we had to drive all the way from the forest.

'Why have you got twigs in your hair Isadora?' asked Zoe.

'Oh!' I said, reaching up and pulling them out. 'I didn't even realize!'

Zoe giggled.

'Where's your friend?' Oliver asked.

'Oh, she had to go home. But she
enjoyed meeting you all,' I smiled.

'I thought she was cool,' said Oliver.

'Yes, so unusual and interesting!'
agreed Samantha.

'Have you decided what you're going
to make for your space project yet?' Zoe

asked. 'Look I've finished mine!' she gestured to her desk where a huge picture lay. It looked just like the Milky Way with glitter and star sequins scattered all over streaks of paint.

'That's beautiful Zoe!' I said, and this time I didn't feel any worry about my own project. I knew exactly what I was going to do! I couldn't wait to get home to start making it!

After school, Mum helped me find lots

of scraps of fabric and some beads and buttons. We sat down at the kitchen table together and started making my project. It took two evenings to finish but by Friday morning, I was ready to bring

what I had made into school.

'Ooh,' said Zoe when she saw what I had brought in. 'I like what you've done Isadora!'

'Thanks Zoe!' I said. 'It feels very special to me.'

We all took it in turns to come up to the front of the classroom and talk about the things that we had made.

'What a simply magical picture Zoe!' said Miss Cherry when Zoe held up her sparkling Milky Way painting for everyone to see.

'Well done! And Bruno that's a very impressive solar system. It must have taken you ages!'

'It did,' said Bruno proudly.

Sashi had made a wonderful cardboard rocket almost as tall as her, covered all over in tin foil, and Oliver had made a papier mâché astronaut's helmet.

'These things are all going to look fantastic displayed in the classroom,' said Miss Cherry.

At last it was my turn and I felt a little bit shy as I stood up to go to the front of the class.

'What have you got Isadora?' asked Miss Cherry.

'I was inspired by what Astrid Luna told us about Glow Sprites,' I said. 'So I made two dolls . . . erm . . . imagining what they look like.' And I held up two dolls— one of Nova and one of Pluto. They both had soft, stuffed bodies and eyes made from buttons. I had tried to make Nova's clothes exactly like the ones she had been wearing.

'How creative!' said Miss Cherry. 'They're charming!' and she took them from me to put in the display. I went back to my desk feeling pleased. It felt nice that the Nova and Pluto dolls would be sitting there in the classroom, watching over me.

That afternoon when I got home from school, I discovered a package waiting for me on the kitchen table.

'It arrived at lunchtime,' said Mum. 'I don't know where it came from. I was in the garden dancing in the falling leaves and it just fell from the sky!'

The package was wrapped up in a

shimmery sort of paper with tiny silver
stars all over it. I ripped it open excitedly.
Inside was something round and yellow
that smelt very much like . . . cheese.
There was a postcard that came with it.

A present from outer space.

Thank you Isadora!

Love, Nova and Pluto

X

Turn the page
for some
Isadorable
things to make
and do!

How to make star ornaments

Nova and Pluto would surely enjoy this unique decoration, and it would remind them of their favourite playground: the starry night sky!

Equipment:

- ★ Cardboard (why not use an old box?)
- ★ Felt pen
- ★ Yarn—any colours you like
- ★ Wooden stick (you could try and find the perfect stick the next time you go out for a walk!)
- ★ Acrylic paint and brush
- ★ Star-shaped cookie cutter
- ★ Scissors
- ★ Glue
- ★ A grown-up assistant

1. Use the cookie cutter and the felt pen to trace star shapes on the cardboard.

2. Ask your grown-up assistant to help you cut the shapes. Be careful—sometimes cardboard is very hard to cut!

3. Paint your cardboard stars and let them dry—you can paint them any colour you like!

4. Put a bit of glue at the centre of your star and place a strand of yarn (between 15cm and 30cm long) on it. You will need to use this later to hang your star.

5. Knot the yarn across the centre of the star to keep it in place and start wrapping the yarn in any direction around the star.

6. If it is a bit slippery, just use a tiny bit of glue to keep the yarn in place.

7. Once you are happy with your star, take the strand of yarn you positioned at the beginning and make a loop at the end of it, big enough for it to pass through your wooden stick!

8. Repeat these steps to create as many stars as you like!

9. Pass the loop at end of each star on to the wooden stick and tie a strand of yarn to the two opposite sides of the stick. You can now hang your starry creation in your room!

You could also paint the wooden stick with some acrylic paint or wrap some yarn all around it to give it a pop of colour!

How to make a starry salt dough garland

The night sky is beautiful, and on a clear night it twinkles with stars. Here is how you can re-create the magic of the night sky in your bedroom!

What you will need:

★ 50g plain flour
★ 25g salt
★ 25ml water
★ Rolling pin
★ Wooden skewer
★ Star-shaped cookie cutter
★ Baking tray
★ Baking paper
★ Oven
★ Glow in the dark paint
★ Paint brush
★ Thread or ribbon
★ A grown-up assistant

Method:

1. Preheat the oven to 100°C.

2. On a clean surface, mix flour and salt and form a little mountain.

3. With your finger, create a tiny crater at the centre of the mountain, like a miniature volcano, and pour the water inside.

4. Mix the flour and salt with the water using your hands, until you have an even dough.

5. If your dough is too sticky, add a tiny bit of flour. If it's too dry and it cracks, dampen your fingers in some water and knead the dough a little more.

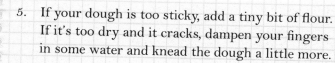

6. Make a small ball and place it on a surface.

7. Roll the dough out to a thickness of around 5mm.

8. Use the star-shaped cookie cutter to cut out the star shapes.

9. Using the wooden skewer make two holes on each side of the top point of each star. Make sure the tiny holes are big enough for your thread or ribbon to pass through.

10. Place the baking paper on the baking tray and carefully move your stars on to the tray.

11. Place the baking tray in the oven and bake for one hour and a half.

12. Take the tray out and let the stars cool down.

13. Now it's time to paint the stars with glow in the dark paint. Make sure you give the paint enough time to dry before moving to the next step.

14. Pass the thread or ribbon through the holes that you made earlier and hang your decoration in a well-lit place. This will allow the glow in the dark paint to recharge.

15. Now it's time to wait for night to come and see your stars gleaming in the dark!

You could also add a few drops of lavender essence to give your stars a lovely calming smell!

How to create your own aliens

As Isadora flies over the town looking for the fallen star, she starts wondering if it might be an alien fallen to Earth. What do you think an alien might look like? How about creating your own?

Equipment:
- Paper plates
- Scissors
- Glue
- Stapler
- Coloured tissue paper
- Coloured card
- Googly eyes
- A grown-up assistant

Method:

1. Cut out a few squares of tissue paper in the colour you prefer.

2. Put a layer of glue all over a paper plate and lay each of the tissue paper squares on top, until the plate is completely covered.

3. Take the card and cut out your alien's features, such as ears, mouth, antennas, nose, etc.

4. Ask your grown-up assistant to help you and staple or glue your alien's features to the plate.

5. Add the googly eyes (how many will they have: one, two, three, or more?) and any other decoration you can think of.

6. Your unique alien is ready to be displayed!

How many different aliens can you think of and create?

ISADORA · MOON

For more activities and information
about the books visit
Isadora Moon on Oxford Owl.
www.isadoramoon.com

For information on the Isadora Moon
animation, check out
the Instagram page.

@isadoramoon

Harriet Muncaster, that's me! I'm the author and illustrator of Isadora Moon. Yes really! I love anything teeny tiny, anything starry, and everything glittery.

Many more magical stories to collect!

Goes on a School Trip

Half vampire, half fairy, totally unique!

Harriet Muncaster

Has a Birthday

Half vampire, half fairy, totally unique!

Harriet Muncaster

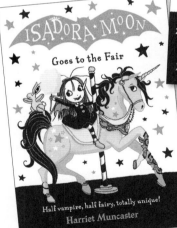

Goes to the Fair

Half vampire, half fairy, totally unique!

Harriet Muncaster

ISADORA MOON
Makes Winter Magic

Half vampire, half fairy, totally unique!
Harriet Muncaster

ISADORA MOON
Gets in Trouble

Half vampire, half fairy, totally unique!
Harriet Muncaster

ISADORA MOON
Has a Sleepover

Half vampire, half fairy, totally unique!
Harriet Muncaster

ISADORA MOON
Goes on Holiday

Half vampire, half fairy, totally unique!
Harriet Muncaster

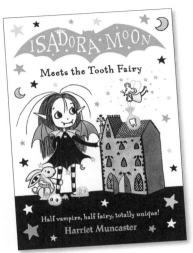

ISADORA MOON

Meets the Tooth Fairy

Half vampire, half fairy, totally unique!

Harriet Muncaster

ISADORA MOON

Puts on a Show

Half vampire, half fairy, totally unique!

Harriet Muncaster

ISADORA MOON

Goes to a Wedding

Half vampire, half fairy, totally unique!

Harriet Muncaster

ISADORA MOON

Gets the Magic Pox

Half vampire, half fairy, totally unique!

Harriet Muncaster

Love Isadora Moon?
Why not try these too . . .